PINGu

and Pinga Stay Up

BBC CHiLDReN'S BOOKS

One evening Pingu and Pinga were playing with
their toys. Pingu was building a big archway for his
castle. He was doing it very carefully to make sure
that it didn't fall down.

Mum was busy reading the newspaper. It was the first time she had sat down properly all day. She was so interested in the paper that she didn't notice how late it was getting.

Pinga had been helping Pingu build the archway, but now she was bored. Before Pingu could stop her, she knocked the whole archway down.

"Just look what you've done," Pingu shouted furiously. "You've ruined my castle."

"I don't care!" Pinga shouted back. "It was a stupid castle anyway. I could easily build a better one than that!"

"That's enough," cried Mum, interrupting them both. "You've done nothing but argue and fight all day. And just look at the time! It's way past your bedtime. Now tidy all those bricks up straight away, Pingu," ordered Mum.

"All right, all right," said Pingu crossly and he stuck his tongue out at Pinga when Mum wasn't looking.

Pingu tipped the bricks back into the toybox with a loud clatter and then banged the toybox lid shut as hard as he could.

As Mum gave Pinga a nice bottle of warm milk, Pingu skated by with each foot in an empty box.

"Stop fooling around, Pingu, and go and clean your teeth," said Mum, firmly. "And don't forget to wash your flippers," she called after him as he skated off.

Inside the bathroom, Pingu sat on the toilet reading a comic. He made a scratchy noise on the side of the bath with his toothbrush so that Mum would think he was cleaning his teeth.

Meanwhile Pinga was sitting on her potty.
"What a good girl you are, Pinga," said Mum,
stroking her head. "If only Pingu would behave as
well as you."

After a while, Pingu emerged from the bathroom looking very pleased with himself. He showed Mum his teeth and his flippers. Mum was too busy to notice that they weren't clean at all!

Pingu was still feeling like having a bit of fun. When Mum went off into the bedroom to make the beds, he saw his chance. He gave Pinga's potty an enormous kick which sent it spinning right across the room.

"Mum, help!" screamed Pinga. "Pingu's pushing me around."

Pingu quickly hid behind the toybox, but it was no good.

"That does it, Pingu," Mum shouted furiously. "Get into bed this minute."

Pingu muttered to himself as he went into the bedroom. But as soon as he got there he forgot about getting *into* his bed and decided to jump *on* it instead.

Mum heard the bed creaking and came storming in.
"I've had just about enough of you this evening,
Pingu," she shouted. "I don't know why you can't
behave like your sister."

Mum began to fuss over Pinga.
Pingu saw his chance to escape,
but Mum saw him slinking off
and called him back.

"And just where do you think
you're going?" she demanded.

16

At last, Pingu and Pinga were both in bed. Mum tucked them in and kissed them both goodnight.

But Mum hadn't seen or heard the last of them. Pinga began to cry for her bottle. Mum quickly went and fetched it and was just going out of the room when . . .

. . . Pingu began to cry, "Mum, I'm hungry." Mum rushed off and came back with a fish for him to eat.

Then there was more crying. This time it was Pinga calling out for her dummy.

"All right, all right," puffed Mum as she popped it in Pinga's mouth.

After that Pingu needed cleaning up.

"What a lot of mess you've made," sighed Mum as she wiped him clean.

Now Pinga wanted her
teddy . . . and Pingu
wanted more milk
in his bottle.

"Mum, Mum," shouted Pinga. "I've dropped my teddy."

"Mum, Mum," shouted Pingu. "Come and pick up Pinga's teddy."

But this time, Mum didn't come. Pingu was baffled. Where could she have gone?

Pingu and Pinga got out of bed and marched into the sitting-room. What they saw there made them stop in their tracks. They just couldn't believe their eyes.

There was Mum, fast asleep on the sofa!
"Why has Mum gone to sleep?" asked Pinga.
"It can't be near her bedtime yet."

Pingu guessed straight away why Mum was so tired. He also knew what to do about it. He went back into the bedroom and pushed the two beds together.

In the meantime Pinga cleaned up Mum's spilt drink.

When they were ready, Pingu and Pinga decided to wake Mum up.

"Mum!" cried Pinga. But Mum didn't stir.

"Wake up, Mum!" yelled Pingu.

This time Mum woke up
with a start and then
yawned sleepily.

"It's your bedtime," Pingu explained. "Come with us and we'll put you to bed!"

But Mum was too tired to move, so Pingu had to stand behind her and push her towards the bedroom.

Soon all three of them were tucked up in bed together and it felt so cosy and warm that it wasn't long before they were all sound asleep.

Other PINGU books available from BBC Children's Books:

Pingu and the Birthday Present
Pingu Celebrates Christmas
Pingu the Chef
Pingu and the Circus
Pingu and the Kite
Pingu Looks After the Egg
Pingu and the Messy Meal
Pingu and the New Baby
Pingu and the Spotty Day

Pingu the Postman Wheelie Book
Pingu Lift-the-Flap Book
Pingu Address Book
Pingu Birthday Book

Fun with Pingu Activity Book
Fun with Pingu Christmas Activity Book
Fun with Pingu Colouring Book
Fun with Pingu Press-Out and Story Book
Fun with Pingu Sticker and Story Book

Pingu Mini Books

Pingu Chunky Books

Published by BBC Children's Books
a division of BBC Worldwide Publishing Limited
Woodlands, 80 Wood Lane, London W12 0TT
First published 1995
Text copyright © 1995 BBC Children's Books
Stills copyright © 1995 Editoy/SRG/BBC Worldwide
Design copyright © 1995 BBC Children's Books
Pingu copyright © 1995 Editoy/SRG/BBC Worldwide

ISBN 0 563 40428 0

Typeset by BBC Children's Books
Colour separations by DOT Gradations, Chelmsford
Printed and bound by Cambus Litho, East Kilbride